The Sleeping Beauty

Plurus

FROM A FAIRY TALE BY
Charles Perrault

TEXT ADAPTATION GIADA FRANCIA

GRAPHIC DESIGN MARINELLA DEBERNARDI

ILLUSTRATIONS BY
Francesca Rossi

Once upon a time, a king and a queen ruled over a distant country with kindness and generosity. The king and queen had been married for years. Their subjects were fond of the royal couple and prayed that they would achieve their greatest wish, which was to have a baby. Doctors and wizards had come from the four corners the country to try to help the king and queen. They each brought spells and medicines, but with no success.

Then one day, just when the hopes of the couple were fading, a fairy who lived in a great forest on the border of the kingdom appeared at court. She told them a secret, guarded for centuries by the inhabitants of the forest.

"The water from a spring in the heart of the forest has extraordinary magical powers," she said. "Have some of it brought to court in a cask made of willow and use it for a long bath. What happens when the queen immerses herself in the water will surprise you!"

The king and queen followed the fairy's instructions. The queen bathed in the magic water and they were astonished to see a shrimp appear in the foam!

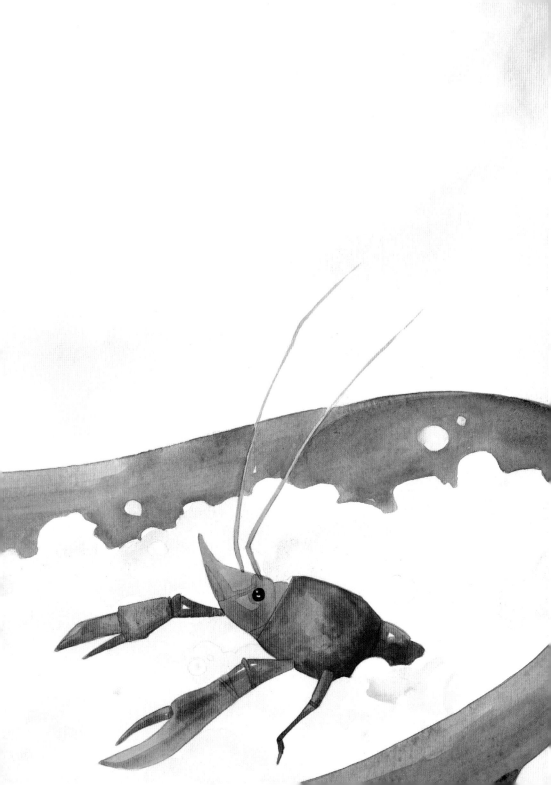

"Your Majesties, do not be so surprised," cried the creature. "As the fairy has already told you, these waters have incredible magical powers."

"But you . . . who are you?" asked the king.

"I am one of the spirits of the forest. I am here to tell you that we have heard your wishes and decided to grant them. You will have a daughter."

The king and queen listened to these words. Just as the spirit had said, the following spring their daughter was born. The king and queen called her Aurora, after the goddess of the morning, because she filled all their lives with sunshine.

Traditionally, heirs to the throne were introduced to the all the nobility and to the rulers of neighbouring kingdoms during celebrations that lasted a whole week.

Soon everyone began frantic preparations for these celebrations. The king gave orders that the castle be decorated with flowers and fruit from the East, that the curtains be replaced with colourful hand-embroidered fabrics and that long silk and satin ribbons be hung in the

gardens. The servants swept and polished every corner of the building and aired the one hundred guest rooms.

A week before the ceremony, the cooks began to prepare the food, and the staff polished the gold tableware reserved for only the most important guests. Hundreds of invitations were handwritten in gold ink, and the fastest horsemen delivered them to the four corners of the kingdom.

The king himself wrote the most important invitations – those for the seven woodland fairies, who had done so much to help him and the queen. There were actually eight of them, but for decades the eighth fairy had lived alone in her cave in the mountains. No one remembered her any more.

Finally the day of the ceremony came. The guests began to arrive at the castle at the first light of dawn. The king and queen received every noble in the throne room, but when the chamberlain announced the arrival of the fairies, the royal pair went down to the main entrance with little Aurora in their arms to welcome them.

During the festivities, each guest went to little Aurora's

cradle to show the child the wonderful gifts they had brought. The last to do this were the woodland fairies. Their gifts were the most precious imaginable – spells that would give Aurora the greatest virtues that any human being could wish for.

"Little Aurora, kindness will be yours," said the first fairy, waving her wand and letting a shower of golden sparks fall on the baby's head.

"You'll be the bravest girl ever seen," said the second, hovering over the cradle.

"I give you generosity," whispered the third fairy, with a slight movement of her hands.

"We give you beauty and intelligence," chorused the fairy twins.

"You will be elegant and graceful. You will dance and sing like no other girl!" said the second-to-last fairy.

It was now the turn of the youngest fairy. She approached the girl with her wand in her hand and raised it over her head. Just as she was about to give Aurora the gift of happiness, a gust of wind blew the castle doors open and a dense black smoke billowed into the room. When the smoke finally cleared, a fairy appeared in the centre of

the room – it was the old mountain fairy that no one had thought to ask.

Aurora burst into tears at the sight of the old woman.

"What's going on here? Who are you?" demanded the king, running to pick up Aurora.

"Is this is the girl you did not want me to meet?" said the old fairy, pointing to Aurora with her stick.

"This is our daughter," said the king. "Who are you?"

"She is one of our sisters, Your Majesty," said the first fairy. "She, too, protected the forest and its creatures before she turned her back on her powers and began to study the dark arts."

"And I have never regretted it, sister! I am a more powerful witch than any of you will ever be, and I will not be ignored. It is an unacceptable insult!"

"I'm sorry if we have given any offence," said the king. "I hope you will forgive us."

"Yes, Your Majesty, but only if I can make a gift to the little princess myself," said the witch with an evil smile. She raised her stick, pointed it at the girl and said, "When she is eighteen years old, the princess will prick her finger on a spindle and die!"

Then the cruel witch wrapped herself in a black cloud and vanished as suddenly as she had appeared, leaving everyone terrified.

The poor queen snatched up her daughter and held her tightly, as if to protect her from the witch's terrible words. "Fairies of the forest," she cried, "Only you can save our child from this terrible fate!"

"I'm sorry, my queen," said the oldest fairy, "There is nothing that can be done to counter a spell of such strength and wickedness!"

"When she is eighteen years old, the princess will prick her finger on a spindle and die!"

"*No one can undo such a powerful spell.*"

Hearing these words, the youngest fairy, who had been interrupted by the arrival of the witch, said shyly, "Sisters, I may have the answer."

"What do you mean? Speak up!" said the queen.

"I am not powerful enough to counter the spell cast on the child, but I have not yet given my gift to the princess, and I can use it to soften the witch's terrible spell," she said. "Aurora, when you turn eighteen, you will indeed prick your finger on a spindle, but you will not die. You will fall into a deep sleep, for at least a hundred years, and from which you will be woken only by the kiss of true love."

When she had finished casting the spell, the fairy turned to the king and queen and said, "I do not know if it will be enough to protect the princess."

The king decided to do everything he could to protect his child himself. That very evening, he summoned his advisers to the throne room and issued a proclamation forbidding any inhabitant of the kingdom to own spindles or needles. All tools used to spin were to be brought to the palace and burnt in the main courtyard.

"This should protect our daughter," said the queen as she stood before the great fire, holding her child.

Years passed and the princess grew into a friendly and intelligent child, just as the woodland fairies had wished for her.

She was also very lively, as her governesses soon found out. None of them ever managed to teach her how to behave like a future queen! One of them said, grumbling, "If only one of the woodland fairies had given you the gift of obedience!"

Aurora loved to escape her boring lessons and hide in the kitchens, or sneak away from important ceremonies to chase the birds in the park, or to venture into the woods. She particularly liked the woods and spent hours exploring trails, picking flowers and chasing squirrels. She would return to the castle with her dress covered in mud, and with pine needles in her hair.

During the long winter days when it was impossible to play outside, Aurora explored the castle's endless rooms.

She thought the old tower, which stood by itself in the grounds of the castle, particularly interesting. Every time she passed it, she stopped to look at it. But she couldn't climb up it – the only way up was by a stone staircase which stuck out from the wall. Aurora was very brave, but she wasn't tall enough to climb the stairs.

"I'll be able to climb the tower when I've grown," she said to herself. "When I'm as tall as that branch on the oak tree I'll be able to." She measured her height every spring and put a small mark in the bark of the oak tree.

There was
only one
place that
Aurora had
never explored:
the old ruined
tower.

The day of her eighteenth birthday came, and everyone was preparing for a huge party. The king and queen woke Aurora with a hug, and then they asked her to be patient. They had to spend the whole morning in the throne room with their guests, but then they would await the start of the festivities together.

Aurora felt bored and began to wander around the castle. When she saw the top of the old tower from the kitchen window, she felt an irresistible desire to climb it. It was the one place that she had never been into. She checked and found that her head now touched the branch of the oak tree – that must mean, surely, that she was tall enough to climb the tower!

Aurora went up to the cracked and moss-covered walls, and put a foot on the first step. She looked up and saw that she was certainly able to reach the second step now. She continued to climb up, as fast as she could. She counted two hundred steps altogether!

When she finally arrived at the top of the staircase, she found a door.

*She ran up
the two hundred
steps that led
to the top
of the tower.*

"That's strange. I didn't know there was a room up here! I wonder what's in it?" she said to herself.

The princess turned the handle and went in.

The first thing she saw was an old woman spinning.

"Oh, I didn't mean to disturb you. I didn't think there was anyone here," Aurora said.

"Come in, my dear. I'm glad of a little company," replied the old woman.

"What are you doing, and what's that?" asked the girl.

"It's a spindle, Your Highness. It's for weaving. Would you like to try?" the old woman said.

Aurora had never seen a spindle before and, curious, she went closer and took it in her hand. But as she did this, she pricked a finger and a drop of blood appeared.

"Oh!" cried Aurora, dropping the spindle. "What's happening to me?" she cried as she suddenly she felt very weak and tired.

"Perhaps you need to sleep," said the old woman with a cackle. She stood up and added, "And so my revenge is complete!"

The old woman was, of course, the eighth fairy, who had returned after eighteen years to take her revenge on the king and queen, who had so deeply offended her.

"I . . . I cannot sleep now, they will be waiting for me at the party. Everyone will be worried," said Aurora in a faint voice, as her eyes closed.

"Don't worry about that, my child. No one will be awake to notice your absence," said the witch.

As she spoke, Aurora fell into a deep, enchanted sleep.

Suddenly, all the people in the castle fell asleep too. The cook fell to the ground in front of the fireplace, still clutching a ladle in his hand. A servant who was carefully

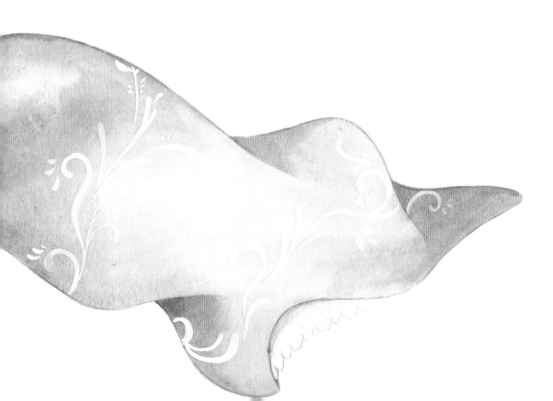

*At the
moment
the princess
fell asleep,
life in the castle
stopped
as well.*

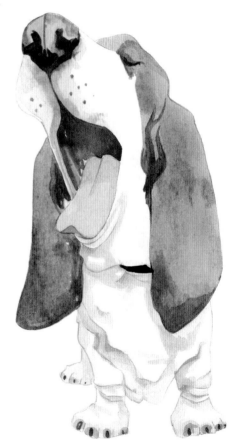

carrying three bottles in his arms, sat down on the steps of the main staircase. A guard leant on his spear and closed his eyes with a sigh. The nobles who had been talking to the king and queen in the throne room smiled at each other and fell asleep clasped in one another's arms, old feuds and disagreements forgotten.

The king and queen were unable to stop their yawns, and they fell asleep on their thrones.

The animals were also affected by the witch's spell. The royal hounds lay down, and the cats who had been scrounging tasty morsels in the kitchen did the same. The horses waiting in their stalls, and the flies buzzing in the stables, all fell asleep. Even the fire that blazed in the fireplace burnt down and the roast meat stopped sizzling.

Every living thing fell silent and slept. An unnatural silence, destined to last one hundred long years, reigned over the castle.

It wasn't long before the courtyards and the paths were covered with moss and ivy. A thick spiny hedge grew around the castle, getting higher and higher, until it

The castle walls
were swathed
in an impenetrable
forest of dense
and spiny thorns.

covered it completely. After a few years, little could be seen of the castle, not even the flags on the roof.

The legend of the Sleeping Beauty, as the princess came to be called, spread far and wide. It told of a princess asleep in the highest tower of the castle, who could be woken only with a loving kiss.

Many knights came to the kingdom over the following decades, attracted by tales of Aurora's beauty and kindness. They were determined to get past the thorns and reach the castle. But none of them was able to do this. The thorns gripped them as if they were the claws of bewitched hands and the knights became entangled and died in misery.

Gradually, people forgot about the castle. No more knights came determined to break the spell, and the legend of the beautiful sleeping princess was a fairytale which parents told their children in winter in front of the fireplace.

Then one day, a hundred years later, a prince arrived from a kingdom far, far away. He had never heard of

Sleeping Beauty. He saw the forest, and intended to go hunting. But as he tried to ride across the forest, he kept coming across a wall of thorns. He tried to see what was behind these thorns and thought he could glimpse the top of an old ruined tower.

The prince went to the village that lay just at the edge of the forest and found an inn. He ordered dinner and asked the innkeeper if he knew about the strange tower that he thought he could see.

"The spirits live there," the innkeeper answered.

"Not at all," said a woman. "It's an ogre's castle! He hides there and eats the hapless travellers that he surprises in the forest."

"Where'd you hear that?" asked the innkeeper, laughing.

"Everyone knows! Only that monster is able to squeeze through the sharp thorns."

The prince was enjoying listening to these stories, when an old farmer sat down beside him and said, "I know what's behind the thorns. My grandfather told me that a very beautiful princess lived in that castle. She was placed under

a spell that meant she would sleep for more than a hundred years, until she was woken with a kiss of love from a brave nobleman."

"A beautiful princess, you say? If the legend were true it would certainly be worthwhile braving the thorns to reach the tower where she sleeps!" cried the prince, smiling.

"Wait, young prince! Don't be too hasty. What I have not told you is that many have tried before you. Some were silly and vain, but among them were some brave knights," the man said.

He continued. "There were great warriors who braved the thorns with their weapons, and wizards who tried to overcome them with potions and spells. Every single one failed and every single one paid with his life."

But now the prince could not help but think of the Sleeping Beauty, and that night he also saw her in his dreams. He had to try to break into the castle, reach the highest tower and free the princess from the spell.

At dawn, the prince left the village and rode up to the thorny hedge. He did not know that this day marked exactly a hundred years since the sleeping spell had be cast on the castle.

When the prince approached the thorns, he was amazed to find that they turned into beautiful flowers. The thick hedge parted, and he was able to make his way through it very easily.

Coming to the castle courtyard, he saw the horses and hunting dogs lying on the ground asleep. On top of the walls, doves were sitting with their heads under their wings. It was so quiet that he could hear his own breathing.

When he went up to the thorn
bush, he found only beautiful
flowers, which parted
as he passed.

The prince walked on the battlements, and saw guards and servants, huddled in strange positions, all fast asleep. He noticed that the clothes they wore seemed very old-fashioned.

He looked at everything in amazement. Then he realised that what he was seeing was a reflection of a day of celebration that had been interrupted very suddenly.

When he reached the kitchens he saw a cook stretching out his hand to grab a kitchen boy, who was running away with a chicken. It was clear that he was supposed to pluck it for a banquet.

In the main hall, he saw nobles and their servants lying side by side. Beside them were the flags that they had once waved and flown with pride. At the far end, on the throne, the queen slept in the king's embrace.

The prince passed them all and headed for the gardens. He found himself looking up at a very high tower. The stairs were steep but he climbed them two at a time. It wasn't long before he came to the top, where he found a closed door.

*The prince ran
to the ruined tower
at the top of which
Sleeping Beauty
awaited him.*

"This must be where the princess sleeps," he said to himself. "Will I be able to break the spell?" He stared at door, not daring to open it.

He finally turned the handle and the door creaked open. There he found Aurora, sound asleep with a sweet smile on her lips.

The prince approached her cautiously. He stared at her serene and beautiful face for a long time. Then he reached out and gently stroked her hair. He was surprised to see that his hands were trembling. Just like a child, he found he was feeling excited and worried at the same time.

Then the prince leant over and kissed Aurora.

Immediately, the room lit up as if the sun had just risen on a new dawn. When the rays reached the princess's face, her eyelashes fluttered and slowly she opened her eyes, yawning. Aurora had finally woken from her deep sleep!

And at that moment, everyone else in the castle woke up. The cook began to chase the young boy, the servant put the bottles that he had held in his arms for a hundred years on the table. The dogs barked excitedly.